Alice
and the
Sea Star

By Gary Murrell
Illustrated by Madhu Greet

First Published in 2020

ISBN – 9798620763887

"We do not inherit the earth from our ancestors. We
borrow it from our children."
— Native American Proverb

Part One
END OF TERM

—◆—◇—◆—

"Three, two, one and...." Mrs Jackson raised a flat palm towards her pupils and fixed them with an expressionless face. Class 6 had known their teacher long enough to understand what was expected of them.

Immediate silence.

She lowered her hand, relaxed then smiled.

"Well, what a lovely leavers' assembly we have enjoyed this morning and I can only add to Mr Jenkins' words by saying how proud I am of you all. Year 6 can move on to Northam High School in September with confidence and excitement about the next step in their learning journey."

There was an end of year weariness in the room, stickiness in the air and plenty of fidgeting. Impatient eyes glanced towards the window while a few heavy heads rested on their desks. Bags packed with exercise books hung on chairs. Oddments of P.E kit and end of year treats had been piled on top. Mrs Jackson's thirty-two pupils just wanted to begin their summer holiday. However, it was clear to all that they were not about to be released to their parents any moment soon. Mrs Jackson had more than just pride in her Year 6 pupils to voice to the class.

"So many achievements this year. Our netball team unbeaten and Josh's fantastic goal to win us the District Schools' Cup," she said then added after a brief pause, "do you remember, Emily?" Emphasis was placed heavily on the girl's name.

A blushing girl in the second row seemed surprised that her teacher could both see and hear her giggling in Lucy Smith's ear at the mention of the goal scorer's name.

Meanwhile Josh, a mousey-haired boy with freckles, lifted his head and beamed with pride. Archie and Sean, his closest friends, turned towards him and gave a thumbs up.

Mrs Jackson was enthusiastic and determined to end the year with a flourish. Clasping her hands together she continued as several pairs of eyes turned towards the classroom clock.

Gradually, Alice in the third row, drifted into her own world as if muffled by sponge packaging. She watched lips move in her's animated face but heard little. Alice's eyes began to close. For weeks the excitement and anticipation of her return to Cornwall had consumed her. Not just during daytime but also through the dark silence of the night. Over and over she had tried to connect again with her secret sea friend, the almigator. She still could not be sure of what it was. A sea dragon, perhaps? Or a cross between an alligator and something pre-historic? But she did not really care.

"And, of course our music concert was a delight," beamed the teacher from beneath a fringe topped by wavy hair. "The choir sang like larks." She paced the floor, a beam of dusty sunlight catching her floral dress. The same dress which she had worn for the concert and on which Rory had spilt orange juice during the interval.

Meanwhile Alice continued to drift, longing for the return of the sleep messages with the almigator. Messages which had last been exchanged nearly a year ago during her summer holiday. She had since squeezed her eyes tightly at bedtime and imagined the softness of its snout and the gloss of its multicoloured skin. She had remembered the fluttering wings and amber eyes and heard the velvet in its voice. Still she worried for the creature's safety. But however hard Alice had pressed her brain no connection could be made. There were no sleep messages. No line of communication. No telepathy as before. Possibly, it was because she lived so far from the sea, she had thought. Perhaps this meant there was no reception like a mobile phone without a communication mast.

Suddenly, Alice was disturbed from her reverie by the mention of her name. She opened her eyes to find Mrs Jackson standing by the class's recycling poster and looking directly at her.

"Last but not least, there's Alice." The class turned towards her just as she was opening her eyes. "Alice, you led our community project this year with so much enthusiasm. Supported admirably by Marie and Eric and your sister, Holly, of course. I think you really have raised everyone's awareness of the problem of plastics pollution."

Mrs Jackson nodded, as if to herself, before bending down and scooping up a pencil which had fallen from her desk.

"Wasn't it fun making recyclable plastic puppets for our school play?" Most pupils nodded. A few exclaimed a weary, "Yes," in unison.

"And I'm sure that the supermarkets and food chains will respond to the petition and reply very soon to your letters. What marvellous ideas you gave them to help reduce plastic. They are bound to be grateful to you. And some burger restaurants have already stopped giving away free plastic toys. Give yourselves a round of applause."

Applause erupted instantly while Alice pondered why it was taking so long to receive any replies. After all, the letters were sent at the beginning of the summer term. The class's self- congratulation only subsided after Rory Banister had stood up and taken a mock

bow to all four corners of the room.

"That's enough, thank you, Rory," said Mrs Jackson while raising her hand for more silence.

"And, finally......." This was Mrs Jackson's third use of the word 'finally' that morning. "Thank you for all your kind cards and gifts. I certainly won't be short of chocolate over the summer. And the pink china cats will take pride of place in my sitting room," she chuckled. Alice was not sure that her teacher was a china cat sort of person. "I look forward to working again with our year five in September and hearing of year six progress at Northam. Enjoy the summer and stay safe."

Immediately, April Harris, a member of the school council stood up, turned to her peers and demanded, "Three cheers for Mrs Jackson. Hip, hip hooray!"

The class warmly obliged. It was now Mrs Jackson who blushed.

A restlessness ensued after the cheering at which point the teacher clapped her hands, restoring order.

At last the red uniformed pupils were lined up at the side of the classroom and led to the front playground where they were met by a bustle of parents and grandparents thanking teachers then waving cheerily as they departed for their holidays. Alice could see Holly holding mum's hand while she talked to April's grandmother. Alice hung back until her classmates had gone.

"Thank you, Mrs Jackson. I've really enjoyed science with you. Well, not just science but everything really. But especially the plastics pollution project."

"You have been a pleasure to teach, Alice and I hope you enjoy your summer holiday. Back to Cornwall, aren't you?"

"Yes, I can't wait. We're going first thing tomorrow morning," replied Alice enthusiastically.

"Are you going with friends?"

"No. Just mum and dad and Holly."

Alice thought for a moment and then continued." But I hope that I can meet with a friend I made in Cornwall last year. A special friend. A friend I've missed."

Mrs Jackson did not respond having been distracted by a beaming father offering her a bottle of wine as an end of year thank you.

Alice slowly made her way towards mum, turning back to face her primary school for the last time as a pupil. I've been happy here, she thought.

But it was time for Northam School in September. And before that a much more exciting and important adventure starting tomorrow in Cornwall. Well, that is what Alice hoped. She smiled to herself, holding her school bag tightly over her shoulder and now running towards mum.

Part Two

HARBOURSIDE

❖

The harbour was impressive with two black cannons guarding its entrance. Enormous sandy stone blocks, although worn and faded in places, stood strong and high, prepared to face raging Atlantic storms. But today it was a gentle sea under a warm sun which rippled into its mouth.

Suddenly there was a loud slap of sea as a young girl hit the water's surface and disappeared, having jumped feet first from the wall. She emerged from below with white bubbles fizzing like lemonade around her head. Other children followed, all in black wet suits as shiny as seal skins. Some suits were flashed with red, others yellow or luminous green.

"Dare you to back flip, Tom," goaded someone. Children screamed in excitement. Tom looked over his shoulder and laughed.

Alice stood by and watched.

Although tired after a five hour journey to Cornwall she had become thrilled by the activity around her. But it was not the sort of place where she would find her almigator. Her attempt to resume their friendship would not begin until nightfall. Meanwhile the harbourside was alive with colour and sound. Canoeists and boarders paddled by while a blue and white crabbing boat chugged back into harbour. This seemed worlds away from yesterday at school with Mrs Jackson.

A few steps below, her younger sister Holly, sat on the sea wall, her pink leggings dangling over the edge. She brushed the sequins on her unicorn sweatshirt with one hand. Pink to mauve returning to pink as mum helped her drag a crabbing net up the side of the harbour wall.

"Alice, look I've caught a crab," she called excitedly as she peered at it closely through the net before shaking it free into a bucket. Alice smiled back.

A little further behind them dad sat on a bench by the Ship Inn drinking beer and reading a guide to fishing Cornish waters. He was already in holiday mood, tee shirt, beige shorts and sandals. A poster pinned to a table next to him warned against feeding the gulls. As if in protest a flock of herring gulls screeched and circled above occasionally swooping low over tourists with pasties, chips or ice creams.

Suddenly, a whoosh of air brushed the top of dad's head as a gull dived within centimetres of his beer. Instantly, he looked up from his guidebook in alarm, covering the top of his pint glass with a hand.

But too late! Splat! A spatter of gull mess missed his beer instead targeting the back of his shirt.

"Urgh!" Dad shouted to the sky as he moved a hand from the glass to his back to feel a warm sludgy slime.

On hearing his alarm Mum turned around unable to resist a grin and then said, "They say it's good luck to be pooed on by a gull."

Alice and Holly laughed together.

"Buy a lottery ticket tonight, love. Your luck's in," mum continued.

"That's why in some parts there be a fine for feeding gulls. Just encourages 'em," said a grey bearded local sitting next to Dad. He wore a black sweatshirt emblazoned with the words, 'Cornwall Native', in yellow.

"I wasn't feeding the gulls. Have you got a tissue, Kate?" Dad did not look amused.

"Not the gulls fault humans feed them," Alice commented. "They have as much right to be here as us."

Dad bent his back as mum wiped his shirt with a piece of paper towel. From the terraces behind them jolly holidaymakers looked

11

down from their drinks, chortling as they toasted themselves under the sun. The black and white flag of Cornwall fluttered proudly from a nearby pole.

By now Alice had returned her attention to the divers who continued to jump from the wall each in their own style; some twisting, others vaulting, a few joining hands in a synchronised plunge. The water looked fresh and clear as it streamed into the harbour. However, a clump of seaweed which curled like green linguine had settled into a fold of the harbour stonework trapping with it an oil tub, plastic bags, bottles and seagull feathers.

"Tom! Tom! Tom!" Three young girls chanted while clapping their hands. A young teenager stood on the very edge of the wall with his back to the sea. He smiled from beneath wet blonde hair clearly enjoying the encouragement. A few seconds passed then without warning he leapt, arched his back, completing a somersault before splashing into the sea. Generous applause erupted from the harbour wall. Alice was impressed too.

Shaking his mop of sopping hair, Tom climbed the rusting ladder, appearing just below where Alice stood.

"Hey, that's awesome," she said as he stepped onto the wall.

Tom did not speak at first but gave her a thumbs up instead.

"That looks dangerous. Don't you ever get hurt?"

He looked at her as if he did not understand the question at first then shrugged his shoulders.

"No. Most of us round 'ere do it. It's brill."

"Really?"

"Mum and dad jumped when they was kids."

Tom, quickly reunited with fellow wet suiters, prepared for another jump.

Alice's dad had settled once more to his beer and guidebook while mum returned to assist Holly in her crabbing. Alice took a step closer to the edge as if to get a better look at the jumpers. They hit the water with such ferocity that her special jeans with llama knee patches and red canvas trainers had become wet from the splashes.

Tom emerged from the sea once more but sat on some stone steps this time. "You on holiday?" The sun caught the brilliant red zig-zag logo on the back of his wet suit.

"Yeah, with mum and dad and Holly. She's my sister over there with the crabbing net.

"My grandpa says you're an emmet."

Alice looked puzzled, wondering what an emmet was. Sounded like a soft cuddly toy. A sort of rabbit perhaps. But the boy explained before she could ask.

"Holidaymaker, like."

Alice declined to comment, not sure whether to be an emmet was good or otherwise. Instead she changed the conversation. "Do you have a brother or a sister?"

"Brother, Sam. And there's Wishbone."

"Do they do jumping?"

"Not Wishbone, he's a ferret. But bit like a brother. Fun sometimes but then a bit of a nuisance. He doesn't like water much and I couldn't find a wet suit to fit him anyway," Tom giggled.

A ferret as a pet, thought Alice, sounded brill.

"Holly and I have got Pudding and Custard."

"Treacle, I hope. You're making me hungry," said Tom rubbing a hand over his stomach and playfully licking his lips.

"Ha, ha," Alice responded in mock laughter. "They're hamsters. Pudding is mine and Custard is Holly's. But what about Sam? Does he do jumping?"

"When he's not on his gaming which he is most of the time. He plays some game about the world fighting a freak storm and floods and disasters and Zombies or something. And he says he wants to be a world champion player. Win a lot of money, be like, rich."

Alice looked unimpressed. "I don't care about gaming. World disaster is real. Plastics pollution. Climate warming."

"Sam says he makes online friends like, who play the games with him."

"Really? I've got an ipad and Dad's just bought me a smart phone. I'm just learning how to use it. But I like to be outside with friends. Riding my bike. Or looking at stars or climbing trees or finding out about creatures. I want to be a marine biologist when I'm older and look after the sea. You know humans are poisoning it with their rubbish."

Tom looked at Alice as if he wanted to ask about marine biologists but instead said, "I like swimming and fishing."

"Dad likes fishing too."

"Grandpa says better fishing like, when he was a kid. The foreign boats come here and take our fish now. Says be better when they can't anymore. Something called Brexit." Tom paused, stood up then laughed. "Brexit sounds like a baby breakfast food."

"My granddad goes on and on about Brexit," Alice replied, raising her eyebrows. "He gets angry, says it's stupid and we'll all end up poorer."

Their conversation was interrupted by an older boy at the end of the harbour wall who beckoned then shouted towards Tom. "Stop gossin' with that girl. Do a back flip with me an' Tracey."

Tom waved back at him and was about to return but hesitated before addressing Alice. "Can you swim?"

She nodded. "You seem to have a lot of fans over there."

Tom ignored her comment. "What's yer name like?

"Alice."

"Well, get a wet suit, Alice and have a go at jumping."

"Mmmm. Not sure. Looks scary. Dad probably wouldn't let me. Anyway, I'm here to find a friend I made last year."

Alice thought briefly about harbour jumping, her cheeks blushing slightly. "What happens if you want to go for a......." She paused. "You know, a pee when you're in your wet suit?"

"You just go if you has to. Just feels a bit warm inside."

Alice giggled, covered her mouth with a hand then whispered to herself. "Disgusting."

Tom threw back his head and laughed before running to re-join his fans.

Moments later Dad appeared beside Alice, book tucked under his arm. "Who were you talking to?"

"Tom. Think he lives here. One of the harbour jumpers. He's good at it."

"Oh, really," remarked dad, disinterested. He wandered towards mum and Holly who were folding away the net and emptying the contents of the bucket. Six or more tiny crabs plopped into the sea their legs wriggling.

Alice's attention had suddenly been caught by a solitary gull. It was standing on a car roof parked between the harbour wall and the inn. It had only one leg. "Ah, he looks so sad but he's lovely," she sighed to herself. It was unlike the other gulls that squawked and swooped and whose feathers shone with metallic brilliance in the sunlight. The one-legged gull stood silently, tatty and with weak, dull eyes.

"Called Stumpy. Fishermen feed 'im. Lost one of 'is legs years ago, girl."

Alice turned around. It was the old man in the 'Native Cornwall' sweatshirt.

"'is an old boy, that gull. But's looked after by the fishermen. Throw him fish scraps. Not that I 'old with feedin' gulls." He stroked his beard then returned to his beer. "'ope I get looked after as well by my missus in me old age," he chuckled.

"He didn't lose his leg in a fisherman's net or fishing line, did he?" Alice looking pained.

The old man opened both palms and widened his eyes. Clearly, he did not know.

Seconds later dad was back beside Alice with Mum and Holly. "Time to find our cottage for the week," said dad looking at his watch. "Not far up the coast. Ready, then?"

"Yes," cried both girls excitedly in unison.

"Don't suppose anyone fancies an ice cream first, though? There's a kiosk at the harbour head."

"We do," shouted Holly immediately as Alice beamed in agreement with her sister. Together the family made their way beside the inner harbour wall towards the town car park, the girls skipping ahead of their parents. A blue haversack hung over mum's shoulder, the crabbing net and bucket in her right hand.

"Sounds quite remote this cottage. I said to the girls we'd be nearer a town this time. Although Alice doesn't seem to mind."

"Only be ten minutes in the car. Cottage is a good size. Got three bedrooms, a sea view and it's cheap to us," commented dad, "thanks to Auntie Barbara. She's only just started the repair work on it, but it'll be fine."

"Well, suppose it's lucky that you've got an auntie with a place here."

Meanwhile, a little further ahead, Alice held Holly's hand and thought about the cottage. The harbourside was full of colour and fun but she could not wait to explore and, of course, for bedtime to come. Tonight, she would try her very hardest to contact the almigator in a sleep message.

Part Three

THE COTTAGE

◆—◇—◆

Seashells, a tiny bird's skull, prickly potted plants peppered with dead flies, wellington boots, a red dog lead, a fishing rod, a pair of binoculars, a butterfly net and spiders' webs. Just some of what met the family inside the porch of the cottage.

"Wow," said a wide-eyed Alice as she pulled her pink wheelie trunk behind her. Mum and dad were directly ahead climbing the bare wooden stairs with suitcases and bags.

"Interesting," Alice thought now standing in the main room. A huge mermaid sculptured from wire hung on the opposite wall while a mantlepiece above an old wood-burning stove was covered with candles in glass jars, hardened wax and pottery ornaments. Dusty dampness hung in the air and there were speckles of greenish mould on the walls.

"Come upstairs, Alice," shouted Holly. "We've got bunk beds. You can have the top one, if you like."

"Coming," Alice called back as she started up the stairs dragging

her pink trunk behind her. Light streamed through a long rectangular window on the landing which was edged with red stained- glass panels.

As Alice approached her bedroom at the end of a narrow corridor, she found Dad standing in the doorway. "Help me with some last bits from the car would you, Alice?" She could still see chalky smears of seagull mess which had dried on his shirt. "You can unpack your case after tea."

Dad examined a tide clock and barometer that hung on the wall in the corridor. "Low tide soon, I think, and weather set fair by the look of it," he said as he tapped the glass.

It was only a minute to the car which was parked at the end of a narrow lane. They had no neighbours other than seagulls, a clattering of jackdaws and a few brown cows. Undulating fields sheltered from the sea by gorse bushes backed onto the cottage.

Dad stood by the opened boot of the car and took a deep breath of air then exhaled. "So fresh and clean," he breathed. "And just look at that uninterrupted view in front of the cottage, Alice."

It was spectacular, she thought and wondered if the almigator might be out there. The cottage stood high on a crag overlooking the bay which shimmered in the afternoon sunlight. To their right rocky cliffs like gnarled giants stretched towards Rinsey Cove and towered above the dark shoreline. In the distance Alice could see

the chimney stacks of old and abandoned tin mines which perched on the rocks. A narrow path snaked its way past the front of their cottage then traced the cliff edge into the distance, but she could see no way of getting down to the rock pools directly below. And this could be a problem in trying to meet with her almigator once again.

"I think we'll all enjoy our week at Sea Star," said dad. He handed Alice a canvas holdall from the car then lifted a second for himself before closing the boot with a click.

"Sea Star?" Alice sounded quizzical.

"The cottage. Its name is carved into the wooden gate before the porch. Come on. Mum's prepared your favourite meal. Be some good star watching to be done here after dark too."

Alice enjoyed the evenings they spent together in the garden at home with dad's telescope exploring the heavens and learning about planets and constellations. If not a marine biologist an astronomer would be a great job she sometimes thought.

Together the pair wandered back into the cottage. A warm and comforting smell of cooking lasagne wafted from the kitchen.

Within half an hour the family had set the table for their meal. Holly busied herself with knives, forks and tumblers while Alice carried a glass bowl of salad from the kitchen. Soon a steaming tray of lasagne was brought in by mum and the four of them sat around the table to eat. They were all hungry after the day's long journey.

"It's really good that we've got rid of so much plastic in our family this year," said Alice.

Both parents nodded, their mouths full of food.

"Paper bags for our sandwiches, no more plastic carrier bags and everything else we've done. But it's not enough, mum. Last week I saw something on tv about plastic in tea bags. We wrote to the supermarkets about plastic packaging in our community project last term. They still haven't written back to the class." Alice wiped sauce from her lips with the back of her hand. "Plastic is not all bad though. Mrs Jackson said it can be useful if it is something called biodegradable."

"Things change slowly, I'm afraid," considered dad.

"But things can't change slowly, dad. And climate warming is really, really, bad too. It won't wait while grown-ups change slowly. I want to join the school protests and marches. Have you heard about 'Extinction Rebellion'?" There was no response from her parents.

She continued and now spoke excitedly. "And we have to eat less meat. I love mum's lasagne, but we could have a vegetable one sometimes. Did you know cows give off methane every time they burp or fart. That's a greenhouse gas."

"It's not as simple as that, Alice. Grass fed British cattle can help reduce our carbon footprint. They live off pasture which absorbs carbon. Cattle production in South America is a real problem, though," said dad.

Holly looked up from her plate and laughed behind her hand. "Oh, Alice. You said, 'fart'. That's swearing, isn't mum? Will she have to go to bed early?"

"Come on, eat up, Alice," mum encouraged attempting to change the subject. "Anyway, what's the plan for this week? What's everyone want to do?"

"Go to the beach and the owl sanctuary," said Holly immediately, putting a hand in the air to get her vote in first.

"I'd like to get out into the bay on a fishing trip. Catch some mackerel for a barbecue," said dad. "Anyone want to join me? There's bound to be trips from the harbour." Holly screwed up her face and shook her head while turning to face her sister.

"Alice?" Mum prompted.

Alice thought for a moment. "I don't know. Explore the rock pools down from the cottage. And could I have a go at harbour jumping, maybe? Like the kids I saw today. But I haven't got one of those wet suits." She looked towards her parents but neither commented. What Alice really wanted more than anything though was to find the almigator.

The last of the meal was completed in silence, apart from the clink of cutlery on china, until broken by Dad's voice. "Time to unpack your trunk, Alice. Perhaps Holly can help us clear the table?"

"Okay," said Holly with a sigh.

Moments later mum and dad began collecting plates followed by Holly with salt and pepper pots. Alice's footsteps could be heard on the creaky floorboards as she disappeared to her bedroom.

"Hey, dad there's some awesome metal sea horses on our bedroom wall above my bunk. I know there's some cracks in the walls and it's a bit dusty, but this place is brilliant." It was nearly eight thirty by the time Alice breathlessly raced down the stairs to find dad in the garden at the front of the porch. Holly was already tucked up in bed being read the second chapter of 'Travels with My Unicorn', by mum.

In the meantime, Dad had taken binoculars from the porch and was scanning the bay. The sea, a soft silver, was drifting in on the tide and covering the rock pools as the orange dome of the sun sat on the horizon colouring the sky with pink, lemon and grey.

"Think Auntie Barbara said the place was built for an artist over a hundred years ago," said dad. "They must have been inspired by these views and seen so much weather. Storms then beautiful seas and skies."

There was a pause. "Ha. I think there are some seals out there. To the left. Just where the sea's breaking. Quite a few of them. Auntie Barbara said she'd seen seals."

"Really? Let me see," said Alice eagerly. "Please." She reached for the binoculars.

Dad passed them to her before stretching an arm and feeling for his glass of whiskey on the small garden table. He had taken several sips before Alice began to giggle.

"Dad," she said, a playful reprimand to her tone. "Have you been drinking too much of that whiskey? They're not seals. They're surfers in wet suits like the harbour jumpers." Dad looked surprised. "But I suppose they do look a bit like seals from a distance and in this light."

"Huh." Dad sat down on a chair and stretched his legs.

Alice turned the binoculars to her right and tilted them towards the horizon. "Isn't nature beautiful? Awesome. Humans can't be allowed to ruin it, dad," she sighed.

Suddenly she stopped, focussing on some movement a few hundred yards from the shore. Then gasped. "Oh, this is different. Not surfers. Definitely. They're jumping. Quite high out of the water too."

"Sounds like dolphins," said dad lifting his back from the chair and reaching for a book which was lying open at a page on boat fishing.

But Alice knew that they were not dolphins. Several moments of silence ensued as she closely followed the sea creatures as they crossed the bay. Dolphins were not many coloured and did not have small

fluttering wings. They were almigators. She was sure. Possibly young ones. Maybe five or six of them. She watched for at least two minutes until they nose-dived and disappeared for good.

"Here, dad. You have a look. But I think they've gone." Alice returned the binoculars. "I'm tired now, anyway. I'd like to get to bed. Maybe I can stay up later another night for some star watching," she yawned.

"Night, Gobberz," Dad called after Alice as she headed towards the cottage. Alice grinned warmly and blew a kiss in his direction. Gobberz, a nickname Dad had had for his eldest daughter for years, and Gremmerz for Holly.

So, there were almigators in the bay, she thought and could not wait to get to sleep. Alice approached Mum, who was now reading a newspaper slouched on a sofa in the main room. She hugged her goodnight and was in her pyjamas then into the top bunk within a few minutes. Holly was sleeping soundly.

The gentle whisper of the sea was the only sound which entered the bedroom. "Oh, I have to focus on the almigator tonight. I must. And there must be a sleep message," she murmured to herself as she nestled under her duvet.

From her pillow Alice could see the dusty sky and the first stars of the evening; most small jewels of light, yet one was larger, brighter and beckoning. She was sleepy but filled with anxiety and at first could not settle. So, pressing her eyes together tightly, she counted imaginary leaping almigators in an attempt to sleep.

And eventually she did. She dreamt for what seemed like hours. Weird and wacky dreams. Laughing almigators in wet suits diving into the harbour, applauded by Tom. Silver seahorses dancing with mermaids who wore stars and coloured beads in their hair while singing to dolphins in top hats. Dad, a telescope strapped to his head, and clapping in time to their voices. But then angry black clouds smothering a steaming and bubbling ocean while fish gasping for breath floated to the scummy surface. Mum wrapped her arms around trees and kissed flowers that were weeping tears into a dried riverbed.

A dream became a nightmare but there was no sleep message.

Part Four

TOM

◆—◇—◆

"You've not finished your breakfast. You alright, love?" Mum bounced through the porch and into the front garden, still towelling her showered hair which dripped onto a stripy summer dress.

"Fine, mum," yawned Alice," just feel a bit tired. I've had dreams for the three nights we've been here. Sometimes I can't get back to sleep afterwards." This was true but she did not mention the mental energy she had consumed trying to contact the almigator. It had left Alice feeling exhausted.

Mum walked over to her daughter's chair, putting an arm around her as she sat down alongside, dropping the towel to the table.

Alice picked up the binoculars.

"You've spent a long time with those binoculars, love. Maybe it's straining your eyes." She paused. "Seen any dolphins or seals?"

"Mmmmm, I don't think so."

"Well, dad's popped into town for some bits and pieces to add to our picnic. Tomatoes and your favourite, olives. Thought we'd take it down to that sandy beach near Rinsey again. What do you think?"

Alice had not really heard her mum as she was thinking about the young almigators she had seen on the first evening. As she focussed her binoculars toward the shoreline, she noticed that the cliffs did not seem so dark today. The morning light had caught patches of grey rock and fiery orange vegetation on the tops.

"Oh, and he is desperate to book a boat for a fishing trip. You know how mad your dad's about fishing. That and special malt whiskies," she added with a smile.

"Yeh, I know." Alice stifled another yawn and placed the binoculars on top of mum's towel. "And his football. Remember, he bought me a Chelsea football kit when I was just four. Had my name printed on the back." Mum raised her eyes in sympathy.

Alice was about to return to the cottage when she was alerted to another presence by the sound of crunching bicycle tyres on the coastal path. She then realised that she recognised the rider.

"Hey, Tom," she called out as the boy drew level with their gate.

"Hey, Alice," he echoed, squeezing his brakes and jolting to a halt. As he dismounted, Alice noticed nasty looking scratches on one leg below his denim shorts which stretched across a knee.

He also had a bandaged finger. Wishbone, perhaps, she thought. She'd heard that ferrets could be quite vicious sometimes. "Got yer wetsuit, yet?

"No, not yet," replied Alice looking at mum. "Mum, this is Tom. He's one of the harbour jumpers. We met the other day."

"Morning, Tom." Mum stood up. Tom shyly raised a hand to acknowledge her.

"Not got your fans with you then?" Alice grinned.

Tom looked down as a pink tinge rose over his cheeks. He did not seem to exude the same confidence as when harbour jumping.

Leaning his bicycle against the gate, he looked up and called out to Holly who had just appeared in the garden. "Hey, Holly, like yer silver boots. Awesome."

She lifted a leg and jiggled the ankle to show her boot to best effect. "Dad bought them for me," she said sounding pleased and then continued, "Alice, is Tom your boyfriend?"

Alice turned and glared at her sister. "No, he's not! He is a boy and a friend. Well, maybe a friend. But you can't call someone you've only met for a few minutes a friend, anyway."

Tom began to turn rosy in the cheeks again but ignored Holly's teasing.

"Hey, come on, you. Let's go inside and start preparing this picnic," mum said as she took Holly by the hand, who then turned her head in Alice's direction as they reached the door and poked her tongue out.

Alice continued to scowl as she returned her attention to Tom. "Younger sisters. A nuisance. Should be sold as dragon food. Anyway, are you harbour jumping today?"

"Maybe, when tides right like. Just biking to me mates now. What about you?"

"Well, we're going to a beach again. It's nice but I've got something more important to do than that."

"Is it like, finding that friend you made last year?"

"Well, maybe." Alice thought for a moment. "Tom, do you know how to get down to the rock pools right below us here?" She pointed to the shore with a finger.

"Think so. Just a few metres along path. But it's a bit hidden. Show you, if you want."

"Okay, but I can't be long. Mum'll be wanting to get to the beach as soon as dad gets back.

Tom left his bicycle inside the garden before leading Alice away across the winding coastal path. They opened a gate which had a notice pinned to it warning of adder snakes in the long grass. Prickly gorse bushes rose up on either side until after about fifty metres where an area of green opened out with a stone cross on the cliff's edge. It was taller than her, painted white and with a chain fence around it and pebbles at its base. The sun shining from behind had cast a golden glow around its edges. Set inside was a metal plate with an inscription:

This cross has been erected

in memory of the many sailors

drowned on this part of the coast

from the beginning of time

and buried on the cliffs hearabout.

Erected March 1949

"Hey, Tom, look at this," Alice called.

Tom stopped and turned back. "Seen it before. Seas really scary round 'ere sometimes. Waves smash against the harbour walls and the cliffs. Boats get crushed. People drown."

"There was a storm when we stayed somewhere near last summer. Brought masses of plastic rubbish onto the beach. I cleared it up with Holly." Alice looked out at the calm bay, closed her eyes and imagined the wild seas and the boats that had been wrecked on its rocks over the years and the sailors who had lost their lives. "Sea's so beautiful here. But it's going to take even more lives when the ice caps melt, and the oceans rise, and storms become even fiercer."

"Come on, just over 'ere." Tom beckoned her further along the path. "You said you hadn't got long."

Thinking of who might have been buried beneath her very feet Alice continued to file behind the boy until he said, "Now, careful here and stay close to me."

They had come to a steep drop where steps had been carved out of the cliff. A rickety wooden rail ran alongside but seemed to be far from secure. Alice followed Tom gingerly, trusting the rail and watching each step. She counted thirty-seven steps to the bottom before they arrived on an outcrop of slippery rock.

There were few clouds in the sky and the sun already felt warm on their faces. Tom pushed the blonde mop of hair from his eyes while Alice removed her sweatshirt and tied it around her waist.

"What's that say on yer sweatshirt, like?"

"'Narwhals. Unicorns of the Sea'. They're whales with long tusks. They're beautiful and they are under threat too. Hunters. Climate change. Warming seas. Disappearing ice and natural food," Alice said despairingly.

"Strange to have on a shirt."

"Well, look at your top." Alice tugged at his red sweatshirt which was covered in sportwear logos. "What's the point of that?"

"You talk a lot about the sea and plastics pollution, climate change and creatures....."

"Because it's so important, Tom. Don't you learn about it at school and read and watch the news?" Alice interrupted, becoming quite heated.

"We do learn a bit at school. And I do like the outdoors too. Swimming and fishing and the sea. And I don't want any of it spoilt."

"Well, there's more to it than that. I'm going to go on marches when I get home and go on strike from school. You should too. And where's Sam today? Still doing his stupid gaming?"

Tom nodded. There were a few seconds of silence broken only by the cries from a gang of gulls as they swooped on a jackdaw before he said, "Sam, says he's going to get super rich by playing games like 'Fortnite."

"Super-rich? Not everything's about money. Stay indoors and have no friends?"

"He says to me he'd prefer to be rich with no friends and live in a mansion and play games and watch YouTube and have online friends. Anyway, he says having friends online is better than meeting people for real."

"Really? Huh, I don't think so," said Alice raising her eyes to the sky.

"Think I agree with you," responded Tom. "But phones and internet are useful sometimes. Anyway, where's this friend you want to meet?

Alice ignored the question and instead jumped down onto a flat boulder. There were only small patches of sand in front of her, yet enormous ragged rock pools draped in brown seaweed stretching to the front, left and right. Possibly some were very deep. She was sure that there were caves set into the cliff faces. Surely, almigators would live here, if anywhere.

Alice cupped her hands around her mouth and called, "Almigator! Almigator! It's Alice. I'm back. Where are you?" Nothing stirred. There was frustration in her calls. Really, she thought that this was a hopeless idea for communicating but three nights of no sleep messages had led her to desperation.

Tom rubbed his hands across his head. "Who's this friend like, called almigator? Weird name. And you expect him to be hiding out there in the rocks like, with the tide coming in? What is he? A fish? You know what you are, don't you?"

He laughed.

"Clever?"

"No, a mad emmet."

"If you think I'm mad you've never met my granddad."

Alice turned and looked up at Tom on the rock above her. She sighed. "It's a long story and a secret. But I need to get back to the cottage before I'm in trouble and mum and dad come looking for me. And you need to bike to your mates or your ferret. Okay?"

"Okay," he agreed. Tom leant forward offering Alice a hand before pulling her up to the outcrop. "You go first, and I'll follow you up the steps. But I still think there's something odd about you."

"Maybe there is. I don't know. And maybe I'll get to see you by the harbour wall later today. Or tomorrow. Or maybe not."

Little more was said as Tom, head down, trailed Alice on their return to the cottage. She continued to think about the almigator. Perhaps it had died from poisoning. Nurdles, it had called the little balls of plastic that collect in the sea. But she was certain that there were young almigators in the bay, at least. She should not have called to it in front of Tom, though. No-one knew about the almigator not even her best friend, April.

They arrived to find mum, dad and Holly throwing a yellow beach ball to each other in the garden. Holly grinned at her sister.

"Just about to come looking for you, Gobberz," said dad.

Alice looked embarrassed as she pushed open the gate and re-joined her family. Tom, on the other hand, appeared confused but was soon back aboard his bicycle and after a brief wave to Alice's parents had disappeared along the coastal path in an instant.

Part Five

TO THE SEA

◆—◇◈◇—◆

"Hey, Alice, come to see the owls with me and mum. You can touch them, and they've got meerkats too. Go on, please," Holly whined, tugging on her sister's arm.

Alice wrestled with her seat belt, eventually clicking herself free. "I'd like to see the owls, Holly, but I said I'd go on the fishing boat with dad."

"But you won't like fishing. It's horrible and smelly. You'll cry," said Holly, adding after a moment, "like you did when you stood on that snail in the garden."

Freeing herself from her sister's grasp, Alice lifted her eyes in annoyance as she stepped outside the car joining dad on the harbourside.

"We'll meet you back here in about two hours," mum called through the open window by the driver's seat. "I think the 'Twit Twoo Sanctuary' closes at 8 o' clock. Have fun, you two."

"And you," dad said.

As the car moved away, Alice noticed her sister making bunny ears with her hands above her head while pressing her nose against the window. Dragon food. Definitely dragon food, thought Alice.

A further evening had passed since Tom had cycled away from the cottage. An evening during which Alice had stood in the garden sharing the binoculars with dad, the sea hissing secrets below them under the silence of the cliffs. They had craned their necks toward the heavens. Endless stars, powdery galaxies, unknown worlds in their shining millions had stretched across the blackness. She had wondered what people and creatures might breathe there. What problems they might suffer. Yet, there was one brilliant light which had intrigued her the most. The one she had stared at through the bedroom window on their first night. Alice thought of it as her sea star, brighter than anything else. Dad said it was a planet: Jupiter. A gas giant, he had said. To Alice it was just magical. The evening had been followed by a peaceful night but again without a sleep message.

And now, next afternoon, she was at the harbourside with dad. Really, she preferred the idea of visiting the owls. She had never been on a boat and fishing was not her idea of time well spent. But if it meant she had a chance of finding her almigator or reaching the young ones, which she had seen through the binoculars, this might be it.

"Over there by the harbour steps," said dad pointing further along the wall. "Just past the ice cream kiosk. That's where he said we were to meet at 6 o'clock." He marched ahead enthusiastically. Alice followed behind his blue anorak which seemed slightly too small for dad.

The inner harbour was alive with small boats, a gentle breeze ruffling the water's surface and singing in the rigging of the larger craft.

"This must be it," called dad across his shoulder to Alice who was looking longingly at the chocolate ice cream cones. He had reached the top of the stone steps and looked down on a boat with a small red and blue cabin at the fore. A pennant with a bird sewn into it hung from a mast which held a furled brown sail. Painted across the side of the craft towards the rear was its name, 'Puffin'.

"Hi," dad called down to a fisherman on the deck.

"Alright? You must be Matt." A face peered up at dad through round glasses.

"Yeah, and my daughter, Alice is just coming. I booked for two."

"Steps a bit slippy. Watch yerself as you come down." The man was short, though broad shouldered beneath his dark green jersey.

Alice now stood alongside dad and noticed too that the

fisherman's face was very round with a close grey beard. His glossy, conker brown head was bald, apart from a few short grey spikes of hair at the side.

"You go first, Alice, carefully. I'll follow." Cautiously, the pair descended the steps which led to 'Puffin' where the fisherman stretched out a chubby hand to help them aboard.

"Like yer sweatshirt, girl. Narwhals, eh? Seen lotsa things in the bay but not seen one of them before. Gonna need that cagoule yer holding, though. Might be summer but gets bit chilly across the water early evenin' time."

Alice settled onto a plank seat at the rear of the boat while dad stood by the front cabin with the fisherman. Her new mobile phone was in her jean's pocket pressing against her leg. Dad would not be pleased if he knew she had brought it to sea, but she had learned that it had a camera and that could well be useful, she thought.

"We'll be off in a moment. Just waiting for me grandboy. Likes to fish, 'e does."

Dad nodded in acknowledgement as the man set the diesel engine into life.

"Got a nice evenin' for it. Calm and dry. Might be a bit of gentle swell though. But should be some mackerel in the bay. Probably some pollack too." The fisherman and dad continued to chat about fishy things.

Alice could feel the reverberation of the engine through the wooden deck boards and looked disapprovingly at wafts of grey engine smoke drifting across the water. Turning her head towards the other side of the harbour she noticed a line of six or seven brightly painted seaside shops and a posh looking seafood restaurant.

Suddenly, a voice drew her attention to the steps and broke the adults' conversation.

"Wait for me, Wishbone!"

Standing above them was a blonde-haired boy in jeans and a red sweatshirt.

"Thought you might have gone without me, grandpa. I had to feed the ferret like, before mum would let me out," he said as he came down the steps too quickly.

"Wishbone?!" Alice shouted out in amazement. "I thought that was your ferret, Tom."

"It's you, Alice. What are you doing here?"

"On a fishing trip with dad but......."

Tom interrupted her as he stepped onto the gunnel. "Well, I named my ferret after my grandpa whose name is Wishbone. It's his boat." He jumped onto the deck and joined Alice at the rear.

"Well, obviously you two knows each other then so no introductions needed there," said Wishbone.

"Well, I'm Matt," dad cut in shaking Wishbone's hand, "and I've seen Tom harbour jumping and outside our cottage talking to Alice." After a brief pause, he added, "Wishbone's an unusual name though." Alice noticed some gaps between the man's stained teeth.

"Well, a nickname I was given years back. Remember when you use to pull a chicken wishbone with someone over the Sunday dinner table?"

"I do indeed," said Dad recalling his childhood, "and the one that got the biggest bit of the bone could make a lucky wish."

"You got it. People said I was lucky out in the bay. Always catches fish, yer see. But I tell yer, it aint no luck. Years of experience is what it is. Knowledge of the sea," said Wishbone, pointing a finger to the side of his own head. "Anyway, time we was off. Help me with them ropes, Tom."

Within a few minutes the boat had chugged its way into the outer harbour, past orange mooring buoys, leaving the high wall to their right where children jumped into the water. The Ship Inn, with a huge anchor attached to its wall, looked down from beyond while the boat rode gentle incoming waves. Alice felt a soft oncoming breeze from the bay on her face and a sense of freedom as they approached the open sea.

"Never thought you'd like want to go on a fishing trip," said Tom sitting next to Alice at the rear of 'Puffin'.

"Don't really. Well, not to fish. Leave that to Dad. But I like the sea."

Tom considered this for a moment. "Wonder if this has got something to do with finding that friend of yours? The one you were like, calling to from the rock?" Tom looked directly at her as he spoke.

Alice avoided his eyes and his question but remarked instead upon the fishing rods resting upright in the boat's cabin. "What

are all those coloured bits and pieces attached to the lines?"

"Lures. Coloured feathers and shiny bits of metal. You reel them through the water. They spin and sparkle and the mackerel chase them because they think they're small fish to eat. Then they get caught on the hooks and we can bring them home for the barbecue."

Alice winced. "Sounds painful for the poor mackerel." She changed the subject once again. "What do you feed Wishbone?"

"Oh, he loves roast dinners, fish and chips sometimes, and a pint or two in the pub." Tom kept a straight face.

"Really? Ha! Very funny," smirked Alice. "You know I meant your ferret."

"They're carnivores so we get dried meaty food from the pet shop. And sometimes he has a bit of raw chicken as a treat."

Alice glanced at his bandage. "Looks like he's enjoyed a bit of your raw finger too."

Tom smiled without comment.

Alice reached for her cagoule before turning to watch the harbour getting smaller behind them. She had enjoyed enough talking for now. It was time to concentrate her eyes on the sea and her mind on contacting any almigator which might be in the bay.

Meanwhile from the cabin, Wishbone steered 'Puffin' further

away from the shore. Dad remained beside him; both seemed to be enjoying the chat.

"This is a treat, Wishbone," said dad after taking deep breaths of sea air. "I work in a tax office all week. Phones, emails, internet, spreadsheets. You know, I'd rather be running my own antique bookshop or growing fruit and vegetables for a living. Just started a horticulture course in the evenings."

"Glad to 'elp get you out to the sea then," commented Wishbone.

"Open sea and a fishing rod; allows some space in your head. Time for some free thought and imagination away from mass opinion on the internet."

"Huh, I've not done much more than run a fishin' boat in me life. Do a few weldin' jobs in the winter. It 'elps to pay the bills." Wishbone sighed. "But I love the freedom of the water. And I see some things out 'ere, I can tell you. Baskin' sharks, sun fish, dolphins. Last year 'ad a real treat. Was out with a trip off Penzance when suddenly there was this eruption of water, not more than say thirty yards from the boat. Guess what.........?"

Dad's eyes widened in anticipation. "Go on."

"This grey shape broke the surface. Big as a lorry it was. Grindin' sound like a steam locomotive. Was an 'umpback whale feedin' on sand eels. Enormous 'e was."

"Wish I'd been there!" Dad was impressed. "What an experience,

Wishbone."

"It was, for me party of fishermen too." He paused for thought. "But there's change in the sea, Matt. Mackerel arrive in the bay later each year. Not so many of 'em either and I've seen shoals of tuna. Shouldn't be in these waters, tuna. Not normal." Dad listened with interest. "Anyway, be turnin' the bow 'round in a few minutes then we'll drop anchor and start fishin'."

There was little to disturb the peace of the sea apart from slapping waves on the hull, the low throbbing of the diesel and the mournful cry of a solitary gull above them. Tom had grabbed his fishing rod from the cabin and busied himself examining his mackerel feathers while Alice remained alert, scanning the sea's surface.

"Look out for dolphins, Alice," Tom said.

"I worry about Alice and Holly in the future, Wishbone. I read that I'm an 'innocent'. Born before the internet. When I was a boy holidays could be boring some days. Television was dull but we had fun playing football, climbing trees, building dens or just staring at the sky. We used our imaginations. We exercised our minds. I don't think we missed out," said dad emphatically.

"know what you mean, Matt. I 'elped me dad on 'is boat in the summer. Learned lots, I did. 'ealthy too. Some days 'e'd take me out in the bay, and we'd fish for hours. If we weren't catching, he'd smoke on his pipe then take out 'is accordion and play. Said music would lure the fish to our lines. Can't remember if it did." Wishbone smiled wistfully for a moment. "Anyhow, me other granboy, Sam, rarely gets out of 'is 'ouse these days. Ask 'im to come on the boat but buried in 'is computer games, 'e is. I tell 'is mum that it's no good for 'im."

Dad spoke up. "Internet is good for some things; information and knowledge, I suppose, but it also fills youngsters' heads with all sorts of fake news and bad things.....my Alice worries too much about the world. Some problems caused by adults that she can't solve. Plastics pollution, climate change. Just want her to enjoy fun with her friends. Not be too serious. Not grow up too quickly."

The conversation ceased as Wishbone slowed the engine and turned the wheel so 'Puffin's bow faced the distant shoreline. Quickly, the anchor slipped towards the seabed, its heavy chain grinding and bumping against the hull as it went. With the engine cut the boat rolled gently with the sea's motion. Alice noticed the sun now sinking slowly towards the horizon in the west and wondered at the beauty of her surroundings.

"Joinin' the fishin', Alice?" Alice shook her head towards Wishbone who was handing dad a rod. Instead she moved unsteadily towards the cabin, feeling the movement of the sea beneath her, and stared through the little window. The others, at the aft, began to fish.

Part Six

THE VISION

—◆◇◆—

It must have been no more than ten minutes after the fishing had begun that it happened. Extraordinary really. There was at first a muzzy fuzz, followed by a buzz then a whistling in Alice's head, as if her brain was being tuned in like an old-fashioned radio set. It was not exactly painful but nevertheless quite irritating. Now wearing her cagoule against the cool of the early evening, Alice sat down beside the gunnel of the boat where she could still see the horizon.

And there they were! She jumped up, brushing her hair from her face. Amazingly, just ahead of her, no more than thirty metres away, jumping from the sea like dolphins. But they were no dolphins. Perhaps there were three, spinning bodies, red and purple and green, two sets of small wings fluttering as they rose above the water until their tails rotated like propellers before plunging beneath the surface. Alice breathed deeply and stifled a desire to yell out in excitement. Instead she felt for her phone, looking for the camera feature before pressing the photo icon as she pointed it out to sea. They are beautiful sea creatures, she thought excitedly. They were almigators.

Briefly she looked towards the rear of the boat. The fishermen, facing towards the shore, were too absorbed in their mackerel to have heard or noticed. Silvery blue and green torpedo shaped fish wriggled from rod lines before being unhooked and thrown into buckets by Wishbone.

"We've some beauties 'ere for the barbecue," she heard him say to dad and Tom before looking towards the sky. "Clouds beginnin' to close in a bit now. Shan't leave it too long before 'eadin' back."

As Alice returned her attention towards the bow, the whistling in her head became high pitched and much less comfortable for a minute before dying away as if she had at last been tuned in.

Suddenly, other creatures leapt like salmon. They were young almigators like the ones she had seen using the binoculars from the cottage.

Then nothing for a few seconds. Had they disappeared so quickly? Well, from sight possibly but instead one, at least, had entered her head. She had been tuned in to receive messages, it seemed.

Just like last summer, when the almigator communicated through the sleep messages, they spoke to her mind. As before, a telepathy. "Alice, go home. Be safe. Our mum and dad died this year from nurdle sickness. Microplastics again. They're everywhere."

"Dead?" Alice's heart saddened. She was in disbelief but found that thought messaging was as easy as last year.

"Dead, Alice. There are more threats for us too. For your family. For us all. Melting ice caps, flooding and storms and poisonous air. It's hard to breathe some days in this soupy sea. So much acid from the carbon. Too much warmth and more disease. Our skin has sores. And it's harder to find our food."

"But the almigator.....I mean my almigator friend is gone, you said? Dead? Microplastics? We've been doing so much at school this year to help get rid of plastics but it's not enough. The adults must do more as well. It's global warming too, isn't it? Things we humans are doing to the land and the sea." She now felt anger and frustration welling inside her and put her head into her hands.

"Something has to change," she muttered tearfully to herself. "Almigators, what more can I do? Can we do? Tell me, please."

Alice waited and waited and just when she thought there would be no more, she heard a small almigator voice. "Alice you and the young and the wise can make the changes. It's not too late. You know what to do." She repeated her question again in the hope of more detail before closing her eyes and lowering her head over the side. Spits of salty sea spray cooled her face as she was rocked in the cradle of 'Puffin'. But there were no more messages from the almigators.

And then she sensed a change. Subtle and possibly undetectable to the others on the boat but a definite difference. She closed her eyes as an eerie silence blanketed the sea followed by a waft of sickly sulphur which caught her nostrils. The air was uncomfortably warm and sticky.

"No!" Suddenly, Alice let out an almighty scream when her eyes opened moments later.

On hearing her cry, Tom dropped his fishing rod and dashed towards the cabin in a panic. "What is it....?" He seemed unable to finish his words.

Next to him Alice's arm was draped over the boat, a hand gently stroking the snout of a sea creature floating on its side, eyes closed.

"Alice, you okay? What is it? Has it bitten you?" Tom stumbled for words as he looked overboard and put his hand on her shoulder.

"Of course not," she snapped. It's an almigator. A young one. They're harmless and friendly and lovely. But I think this one is dead," she went on, beginning to weep but still petting it's smooth body. "Like his parents."

"The friend you were looking, for?" The boy leaned over the side and examined the creature, his eyes wide in amazement. "Like a small colourful winged dolphin, sort of alligator, dragon like thing."

Alice nodded. "I'd made friends with one of its parents last year."

"Grandpa, you ever seen anything, like this?" Tom said bewildered as both he and Alice turned their heads towards the adults.

But there was no response. It was ridiculous. How could the adults not feel the difference in the air? Not smell, it? It was if the children were there alone, enclosed in a world which had been abandoned to them by adults and did not belong to them anymore. Instead both Wishbone and dad were sleeping deeply and peacefully in their seats. As if they were having an old people's snooze after a Sunday dinner, stuffed with roast potatoes and meat and content with their lot. Their heads slumped on their chests, hands still holding fishing rods, oblivious to this new world. Next to them buckets of shimmering mackerel.

Alice pulled herself up from the side of the boat. They were about to approach the sleeping men when instead they were fixed by a further change all around them. They felt unable to move, their legs like buckets of cement.

"What's going on now? It's too murky for early evening too. And there's an awful pong from the sea."

"I don't know, Tom," said Alice as they stood side by side next to the cabin, "You're the sea boy. You tell me. But it's really scary."

Suddenly, the sun had disappeared completely, and the sky

blackened while the distant cliffs seemed to dance under orange fire. At the same time mist began to rise from the depths of the sea as 'Puffin' rocked unsteadily on steamy water. There was no calling from sea birds. Fish and other sea creatures, never seen by Alice or Tom, floated to the surface, their mouths working as they gasped for air. The salty water bubbled with oily red and green froth like a witch's cauldron and 'Puffin' felt as if she was rising on a rotting sea but tilted by the weight of her anchor. And as if not frightening enough, wailing cries like the voices of dead souls drifted on a lifting wind.

"I'm frightened, Tom. Why can't the grown-ups see what's happening? Just sleeping like babies through all this they are," said Alice grabbing hold of Tom's arm.

Tom tensed before pulling himself free from her grip. "I don't know. Reckon it's your fault, emmet. You and those weird creature friends of yours. Like it's some sort of curse you brought on us by talking to them. Go swim with yer almigtor."

The almigator, thought Alice. She peered overboard to see the tail of the dead creature disappearing beneath the gurgling surface.

They both held tightly to the cabin as the wind wrapped shrouds of mist about them.

"Even the air tastes bitter," gasped Tom, "like it's poison. And it feels sticky and warm inside this sweatshirt and I'm thirsty."

"Something a bit like this happened to me last year."

"You what? Wish you'd said before," Tom shook his head in astonishment. "You're really someone to avoid. I don't want to die at sea and be one of those people remembered by that cross on the cliff!"

"Look," said Alice, "let me hold onto you and we'll go to the back of the boat together and shake them awake. Wishbone and dad will know what to do; they're adults." But neither of the children could move either through frozen panic or..... who knew what?

But then moments later, just as horror had held them, something else was soon to be their release.

"Look up," breathed Alice.

From above them, and a little to the south, there was a light breaking through the dark sky, but it was not the moon. The angry clouds parted to leave just enough hazy space for this brightness. It was shining more brightly than any star Alice had ever seen before. Shining with a purity, from far away, it cleared the filth. Could it be Jupiter, she thought? My sea star beaming on, us?

"Shall we make a wish? Even without a wishbone?" Alice said with uncertainty, turning to Tom.

"Just wish we'd get back home," replied Tom.

There was a brief silence before Alice made her own secret wish.

The clouds melted further as the star shone even more brightly and an evening light began to replace the gloom. The sea settled to a gentle swell, the poisons suffocating its surface disappeared with the creatures and the fish and the air cleared. No more ghostly wailings. From directly above them a solitary gull landed on the cabin roof. It turned to fix Alice with a stare. It had only one leg.

"Stumpy," she said now more cheerfully, "I'm pleased to see you. Come to rescue us?"

"Stumpy?" A deeper voiced echoed from the rear of 'Puffin'. "That gull's flown over from the 'arbour. Can smell our fish."

Both Wishbone and dad turned towards the cabin to see the children looking at the gull. The men were still holding their rods but sitting upright. For them it was as if nothing had happened. Clearly, they had not felt any of this catastrophic world. Instead they had been in their world, comfortably asleep, it seemed.

"Think we've enough mackerel and it's about time we were 'eadin' off back. You ready, Matt? Put those rods back up front, would yer? See you've 'ad enough fishin' too for today, Tom. Seen any dolphins? I miss anything interesting?"

Tom and Alice looked at each other but did not comment. What were they to say?

"Don't know about you, Matt but I think I drifted off for a

little forty winks. Never nodded off before on a fishin' trip. Bit worrying, though. Must be me age, I suppose. Can't beat a rest though at my age."

"Strange, feeling. Can't even remember drifting off," said dad. "Must be overtired or it's all this fresh sea air." Dad put down his rod, stood up, stretched and yawned.

"Is that Jupiter shining so brilliantly this evening, dad?"

Dad lifted his head. "Could well be, Alice. Must say, it's particularly bright tonight. Looks as if it's come to guide us home."

Alice and Tom moved towards the rear of 'Puffin' and resumed their wooden seats. Alice lifted her head towards the star once more while Tom, still in shock, stared at the sea.

"Never been so scared," he whispered to Alice. "Sure, it wasn't all a dream?"

Alice looked him calmly in the face and shook her head. "Not a dream, Tom. More like a real nightmare. A vision of the future."

As dad stacked the rods into the cabin, Wishbone spent a good ten minutes trying to start the diesel engine. It coughed and spluttered but refused to catch. "Well, in all my years I've never known me reliable old diesel to be so stubborn." Bent over the mechanism, with his bottom pointing at the sky, he scratched his head. "Can't beat diesel, though."

Wishbone lifted his head from the engine, returned a spanner to his toolbox and wiped his oily hands on a rag.

"Well, nothin' for it but to unfurl the old sail. Fortunately, wind got up a tad while we was asleep so we'll be back before long."

Victory for wind power, cleaner than your diesel, thought Alice.

Soon the anchor was winched aboard, and all was set. Puffin enjoyed a peaceful sail towards land with the wind whistling in her rigging and flapping her sail. Stumpy remained on the roof, eying the mackerel bucket. With the harbour entrance in full view dad turned to Alice while looking at his watch.

"Nearly half past eight. Mum will be starting to worry about us, Gobberz. Wish I had my phone. Think we're close enough to land now for it to work." Dad was pointing at a tall communication mast on a mound, just beyond the harbour.

"Try my mobile," said Alice, pulling her phone from a pocket.

Dad said nothing, instead looking disapprovingly at his daughter for a moment, before taking the phone and ringing mum.

"Well, 'ope you enjoyed the trip, Matt," said Wishbone shaking dad's hand. They were moored by the harbour steps now. "Got enough mackerel for a good barbecue tomorrow. And nice to meet you too, Alice. I 'ope you weren't too bored today. Perhaps you'll come out with us again, sometime."

Alice smiled. "Not boring, Wishbone. Really wasn't boring."

Dad said his farewells then carried a string of fish up the stone steps and wandered towards the car.

"And good luck with the 'orticulture," Wishbone shouted after him. Dad turned and waved in acknowledgement.

Meanwhile Alice stood with Tom outside the closed ice cream kiosk. They had talked little on the return trip to the harbour. Both were still shocked and trying to understand their experience.

"Sorry I got a bit of a strop like out there. I was just so scared, and I'm really confused about what's going on," he said looking at his feet. "And those almigator creatures. They're real aren't they? We didn't just imagine them?" Tom paused. The only response was a frown on Alice's brow. "Well, where do they come from then?"

Alice shrugged her shoulders.

"Do you think it means we've got to do more. I mean you and me? Maybe that's why we saw things today," said Tom.

"Well, I can't just forget what happened out there, Tom. Leave it all behind in Cornwall. Climate change is bad for everyone. Too much carbon in the sea. Warming oceans. Destruction of forests. Disease, storm damage, flooding, shortages of food and hunger. That's what's going to happen." Alice was animated.

"I know. I have seen quite a bit on the news. Always flooding somewhere. People being rescued in boats and houses full of mucky water," said Tom.

"Have you seen what's happening in Australia?" Tom nodded in response. "I've relatives out there. It's getting hotter and hotter with more and more bush fires. Wildlife destroyed and people losing their homes and lives and smoke suffocating the cities," Alice talked more quickly before falling silent.

Tom had become overwhelmed by the evening and tried to change the subject. "Do you want to try some harbour jumping, then?"

Another pause followed before Alice sighed. "Not this holiday. I've had enough adventure with the water for now. Anyway, we're going home after tomorrow and I've not persuaded mum and dad to buy me a wetsuit, yet."

"Pity."

"But I think you're going to be hearing a lot more about climate change. And I'm going to get involved more once I get home. Adults have got to listen. And do much more. And we must protest until they do. You should too, Tom."

Alice reached for her pocket again. "If you put your number into my phone, I can message you about it."

It was Tom's turn to shrug his shoulders. "Okay, if you like." He took the phone from her, then sneakily pressed on the photo gallery. And if proof were needed it was there. A photograph of colourful, winged almigators leaping from the sea. Tom sighed before clicking to the address page.

As he was recording his number, Alice looked towards a small shop by the roadside which sold groceries, buckets, spades, wetsuits and souvenirs. An enormous plastic shark hung in the window displaying hideously sharp teeth. Propped up outside was an advertising poster for local newspapers. In bold black letters it read:

"Now or Never to Fight Global Warming"

Alice thought. Doesn't sound great. Frightening, really. Her attention was soon distracted by both Tom holding the phone towards her and Dad's voice calling from the harbour head.

"Come on, Alice. Mum's waiting."

Alice accepted her phone and slipped it into her pocket. Immediately, she walked towards the car before turning back after a few paces. Tom was now standing by the roadside with a blonde-haired woman she assumed to be his mum. She was holding a ferret by a lead.

"Bye, Tom. And not too many pints of beer for your ferret," she shouted to him laughing, and gave a wave goodbye. Both Tom and his mum returned Alice's wave before moving away.

As she reached the car, Alice found Holly greeting her with a furry toy owl.

"Look, Alice. He's called Mister Wise. He's mine. Do you like him? And I've bought an owl pencil case for you."

"Ah, thanks Holly. That's nice. Dad's brought you a smelly mackerel," said Alice. "Shall we go home now? I'm pretty tired."

Holly did not look impressed by the fish. "I bet 'Twit Twoo' was more exciting than a silly fishing trip," said Holly.

"More exciting? Maybe," remarked Alice as she climbed into the back seat and fastened her belt. "Or maybe not." With eyes closed she snuggled her head against Holly's shoulder and fell asleep.

Other Books by Gary Murrell

Hooky Cooky Ollie.

Alice and the Almigator.

The Christmas Journey.

Printed in Poland
by Amazon Fulfillment
Poland Sp. z o.o., Wrocław